Published in 2018 by Groundwood Books / House of Anansi Press
groundwoodbooks.com
This edition of *Bitter and Sweet* was printed for PJ Library in 2018
Second printing 2022
ISBN 978-1-77306-234-1

Groundwood Books is grateful for the opportunity to share stories and make
books on the Traditional Territory of many Nations, including the Anishinabeg,
the Wendat and the Haudenosaunee. It is also the Treaty Lands of the Mississaugas
of the Credit. In partnership with Indigenous writers, illustrators, editors
and translators, we commit to publishing stories that reflect the experiences
of Indigenous Peoples. For more about our work and values, visit us at
groundwoodbooks.com.

We gratefully acknowledge for their financial support of our publishing program
the Canada Council for the Arts, the Ontario Arts Council and the Government
of Canada.

Canada Council   Conseil des Arts
for the Arts   du Canada

ONTARIO ARTS COUNCIL
CONSEIL DES ARTS DE L'ONTARIO
an Ontario government agency
un organisme du gouvernement de l'Ontario

With the participation of the Government of Canada   Canadä
Avec la participation du gouvernement du Canada

0123/BI327/A6

The illustrations were done in collage and oil paint on gessoed watercolor paper.
Design by Michael Solomon
Printed and bound in South Korea

FSC
www.fsc.org

MIX
Paper from
responsible sources
FSC® C013572

For Dan, who makes the world
a sweeter place. — SVF

For Roslyn and Charlie,
our newest family members.
Welcome to the world! — KB

Bitter
and Sweet

Sandra V. Feder

Pictures by Kyrsten Brooker

GROUNDWOOD BOOKS
HOUSE OF ANANSI PRESS
TORONTO / BERKELEY

Hannah didn't want to move.

   She loved her house with the wide porch, her
street that was perfect for bike riding, and her
school with all her friends.

But her father had a job in a new town. "Almost every change has some hard parts and some nice parts," her grandmother said when Hannah called to tell her the news. "I was scared when my family left the old country, but we made a new life and I made new friends. Definitely some bitter but even more sweet."

Hannah tried to think about the good things that the move might bring. She tried, like her grandmother, to think of sweetness. But as her family prepared to leave, she could only feel the bitter.

YARD SALE

She cried salty tears when she hugged her friends goodbye and when her teacher took all her artwork down from the classroom walls.

Her tummy felt tight as she helped her parents
pack up her room and as she saw the boxes put onto
the big truck.

"Some bitter but even more sweet," she heard her
grandmother saying.

"Grandma must be wrong," Hannah thought as she watched the town where she was born disappear from sight. "There's nothing sweet about leaving everything I know."

Soon the family was in their new home in their new town.

Hannah's bed didn't fit neatly by the window. Her artwork looked lonely on the walls.

The new house was on a hill, which was not easy
for bike riding, and the porch was smaller.
"Only the bitter," Hannah said.

When their first week neared its end, Hannah
watched her mother light the Shabbat candles. She
was surprised by how nice the new house looked in
the soft light.

As she tasted the sweet grape juice, she
remembered her grandmother's words — some
bitter and some sweet.

But still Hannah wondered whether she would
ever feel the sweet the same way that she had before.

On Sunday morning, there was a knock on the
door. A girl who appeared to be about Hannah's age
stood on the narrow porch holding a small bag.

"Hi, I'm Maya," she said, handing Hannah the
bag. "I live down the street."

Hannah looked inside and saw cocoa powder.

"It makes the best hot chocolate," Maya
promised as she waved goodbye.

"Thank you," Hannah called, feeling better
than she had in a long time as she watched
Maya head home.

Hannah went inside to
heat up some milk.

She carefully added a tablespoon
of cocoa powder and stirred until
the mixture was silky smooth.

Then she took a big, rich sip.
"Ptooey!" The brown liquid flew out of her mouth.
"It's bitter!" Hannah cried. "Just like everything else."

The next day at school, Hannah tried to avoid
Maya. But at recess, Maya ran right up to her.

"I forgot to tell you," Maya said. "You have to
add sugar to the cocoa otherwise it's —"

"— bitter," Hannah said, finishing Maya's
sentence.

Hannah raced home after school to try again. She heated the milk and added the cocoa, but this time she also put in a big, heaping tablespoon of sugar.

"Mmm," she said, taking a sip. It wasn't bitter anymore, but still something was missing. Hannah looked out the window.

She ran out the door, biked down the hill and knocked on Maya's door.

"Want to come over for hot cocoa?" she asked.

"Sure," Maya replied. "Let's drink it on your porch. You have such a nice one."

That night Hannah called her grandmother.

"I thought it was only bitter here," Hannah said.

"And did you find the sweet?" her grandmother asked.

"Oh, Grandma," Hannah said. "You can't just find it. You have to add it yourself."

AUTHOR'S NOTE

In writing this story, I was inspired by the wisdom of many Jewish traditions that contain elements of both sweet and bitter, or happy and sad. While use of the phrase — bitter and sweet — is my own way of acknowledging this duality in everyday life, Judaism and Jewish teachings provide many wonderful ways to see that life holds some of both.

In Jewish tradition, many happy moments are marked with something sweet. Sweet wine or grape juice is used to welcome Shabbat on Friday nights, and at Rosh Hashanah apples are dipped in honey for a sweet New Year. At the same time, Judaism does not shy away from acknowledging the difficulties of life. During the Passover Seder, even as the joy of freedom is being celebrated,

bitter herbs are eaten to remind all of the bitterness of slavery. At the end of a beautiful wedding, the groom breaks a glass as a reminder both of the destruction of the Temple in Jerusalem and the fragility of love. Then, right after the glass is broken, guests shower the couple with the words "mazal tov," an expression of heartfelt congratulations, returning at the end of the ceremony to the sweet.

While Judaism acknowledges that life is indeed filled with moments of both bitter and sweet, it also teaches an abiding sense of hope and obligation — to celebrate the good and be part of creating the sweet.